Santa's Sick of Cookies

An Eastern Shore Christmas Tale

Written by **Karen Young Foley**

Illustrated by **Jessica Gibson**

BELLE ISLE BOOKS
www.belleislebooks.com

ISBN: 978-1-947860-27-8
LCCN: 2018955043

Design and production management by Abigail Montiel

Printed in the United States of America

Published by Belle Isle Books (an imprint of Brandylane Publishers, Inc.)
5 South 1st Street
Richmond, Virginia 23219
belleislebooks.com | brandylanepublishers.com

BELLE ISLE BOOKS
www.belleislebooks.com

To my parents, George and Rose Young

Willis Wharf harbor sits snugly **aglow**,
hugged by soft **moonlight** and Christmas Eve **snow**.

Santa flies **South** from a Pole far **away**
as Eastern Shore **youngins** keep watch for his **sleigh.**

Brittany B

I read **Yuletide** tales from my perch on Gramp's **knees** about **wide-eyed** tots leaving Santa **cookies.**

They leave **lemon** drops and sweet raisin **bars** and **raspberry** cookies all shaped like **stars**.

Snickerdoodles and oatmeal **crunches,**
cookies, **cookies** baked by the **bunches.**

Down every brick chimney, the same sugary sight
Chincoteague Island to Bayford, more cookies to bite –

Peanut **butter**, chocolate **chip**,
cream-**filled** and homemade **jelly**,

coconut **puffs**, shortbread **squares**,
thin mints **round** as his **belly**.

I bet Santa's **sick** of cookies by **now**,
but an **empty** plate I cannot **allow**.

Should I serve peach **pie** or Smith Island **cake**,
a peppermint **stick** or a cold **milkshake?**

Figgy **pudding** might drip on Santa's red **suit**
or **splatter** below on his shiny black **boots.**

No crumbly, old **cookies**, I know what I'll **do**;
I can leave Santa Claus our local **seafood**!

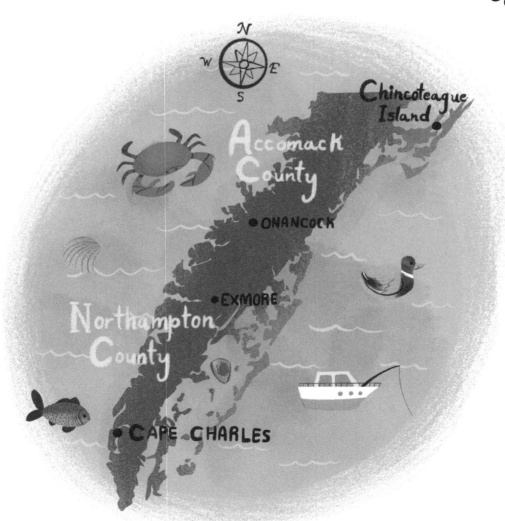

Maybe Broadwater **salts** from the **seaside** or little neck **clams**... I just can't **decide!**

No soft shell **crabs** for a very good **reason**— creeks are iced **over**, so they're out of **season**.

Oysters are **nestled** in their Hog Island **beds** while visions of **pearls** dance through their **heads.**

I'll need **magic** to find a single clam **fritter**.
And one's not **enough**—I need a whole **litter!**

It's too late to **drop** a line off the **dock.**
St. Nick will land **soon.** I'm racing the **clock.**

Unable to **slumber**, no seafood in **hand**,
I give up and **reach** for a gingerbread **man.**

LOOK!

Dad's fresh **baysides**—clean and shucked as **well**—
a platter of **oysters** on the half **shell.**

"I'm one smart **cookie**." I gleefully **grin**,
placing **Tabasco** by our tree in the **den**.

Santa will **love** this special Christmas **dish**,
and **next** year I'm fixing to fry him a **fish!**

Recipe for Santa's Oysters on the Half Shell

1 dozen fresh oysters in shells

Tabasco® sauce

black pepper

lemon wedges

crushed ice

Scrub oyster shells with cold water to remove any grime.

Open and drain the oysters. Discard liquid and top shell.

Chill the oysters in their deep shells on a bed of crushed ice.

Sprinkle each oyster with Tabasco® sauce, black pepper, and lemon juice, as preferred.

Glossary

Bayford: A small village on Nassawadox Creek.

Baysides: Oysters grown along the Bay side of the Eastern Shore.

Broadwater salts: A local brand of oysters.

Chincoteague Island: A National Wildlife Refuge known for the annual pony swim and auction.

Hog Island: One in a line of barrier islands providing a buffer between the Eastern Shore and the Atlantic Ocean.

Smith Island cake: Named after an island in the Chesapeake Bay, this yellow cake with 10 or more pancake-thin layers is frosted inside and out with chocolate fudge icing and sits only 3 inches tall. Wives originally baked the cakes for their watermen leaving for the autumn oyster harvest.

Willis Wharf: A seaside town that is home to local aquaculturalists.

About the Author

Karen Young Foley has fond memories of leaving cookies for Santa. She was born and raised on the beautiful Eastern Shore of Virginia, where the bay meets the sea. A Phi Beta Kappa graduate of the University of Virginia, she is a National Board Certified Teacher and member of Delta Kappa Gamma International Society for Key Women Educators. She resides on the Chesapeake Bay with her husband Jack and their yellow lab, Gunner.

About the Illustrator

Jessica Gibson is a freelance illustrator based in Detroit, Michigan. Art has always been her passion, and she started doing it professionally in 2016. Her artwork has been featured in many children's books and other related media, editorials, and games.

CPSIA information can be obtained
at www.ICGtesting.com
Printed in the USA
LVHW062138101118
596704LV00004B/15/P